Drawing THINGS WITH WINGS

A STEP-BY-STEP FUN GUIDE

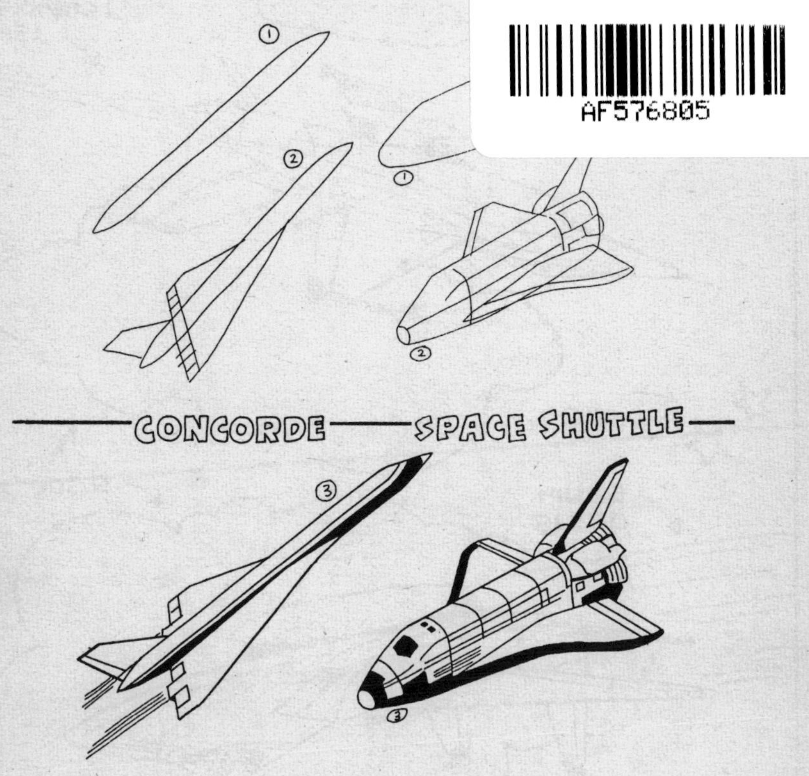

Published by: **Watermill Press**
Mahwah, New Jersey

ISBN 0-8167-1669-2

Manufactured in the United States of America

PLACING YOUR DRAWING IN A SETTING WILL MAKE YOUR PICTURE MORE INTERESTING.

DRAWING TIPS

ALWAYS DRAW THE FIRST **2** STEPS LIGHTLY IN PENCIL UNTIL YOU ARE PLEASED WITH THE WAY IT LOOKS.

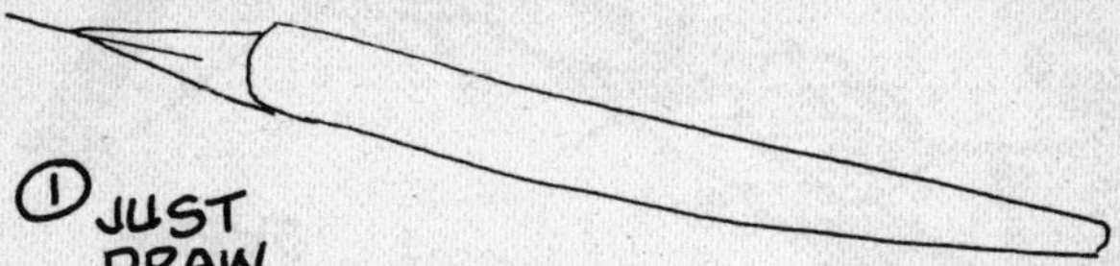

① JUST DRAW BASIC SHAPES

DON'T BE AFRAID TO ERASE!

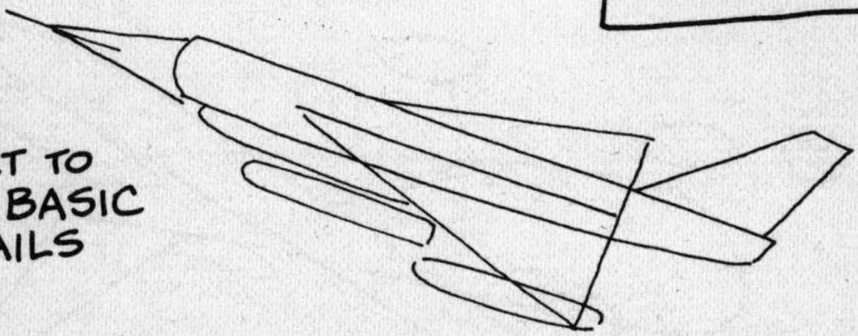

② START TO ADD BASIC DETAILS

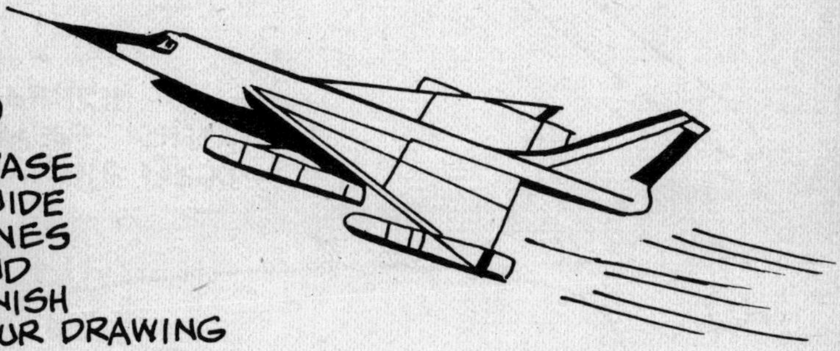

③ ERASE GUIDE LINES AND FINISH YOUR DRAWING

ADD DETAILS SUCH AS FLAPS, BLACK AREAS, SPEED LINES AND BACKGROUNDS ONLY AFTER YOU'VE COMPLETED THE FIRST **2** BASIC STEPS. ***HAVE FUN!***

CESSNA

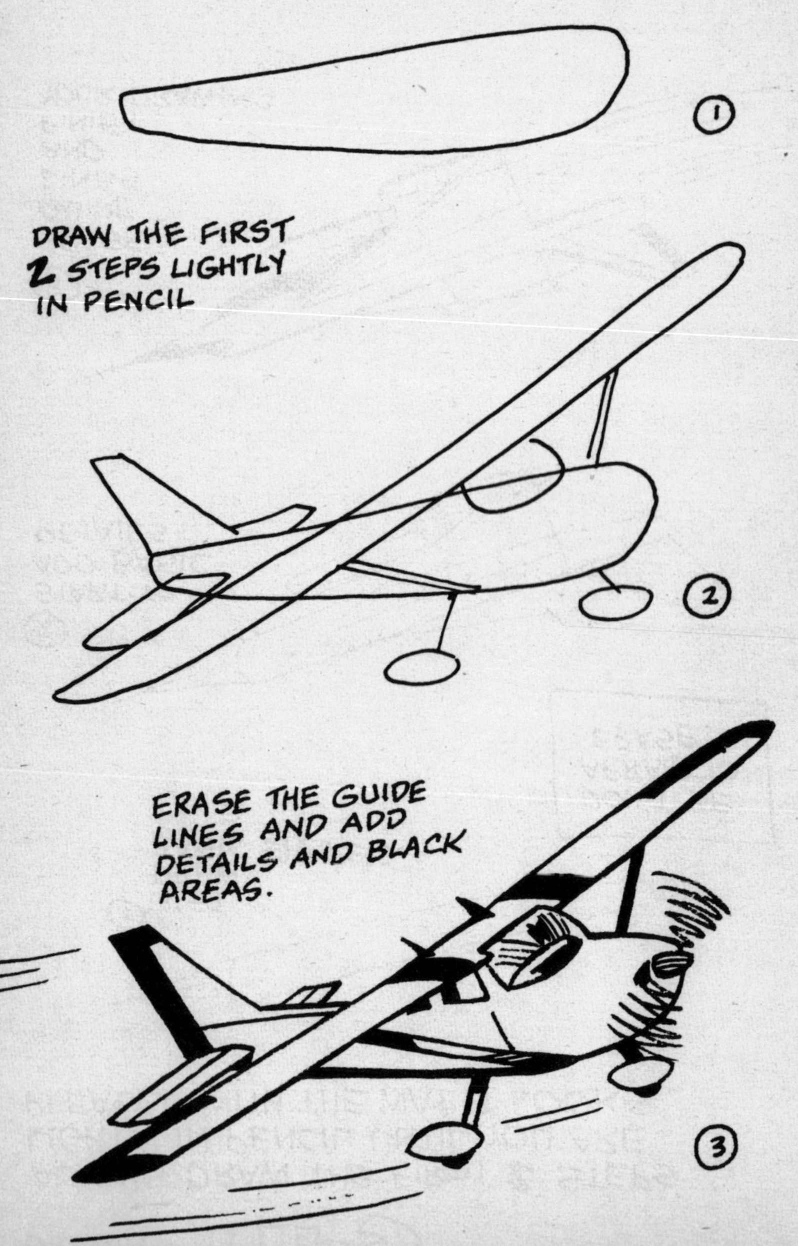
1
DRAW THE FIRST
2 STEPS LIGHTLY
IN PENCIL
2
ERASE THE GUIDE
LINES AND ADD
DETAILS AND BLACK
AREAS.
3

F-15 EAGLE

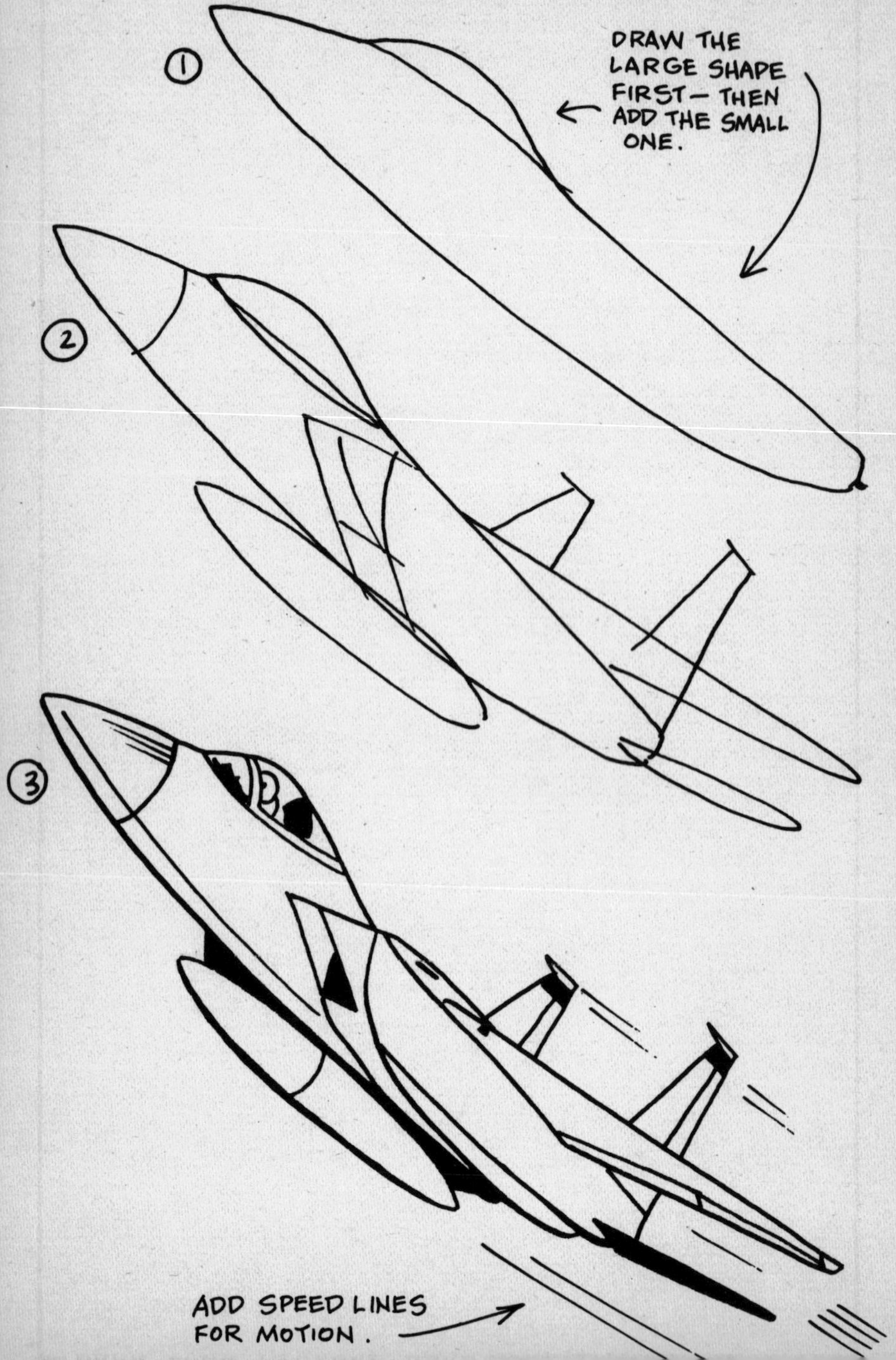

1

DRAW THE LARGE SHAPE FIRST— THEN ADD THE SMALL ONE.

2

3

ADD SPEED LINES FOR MOTION.

DRAW YOUR PICTURE HERE

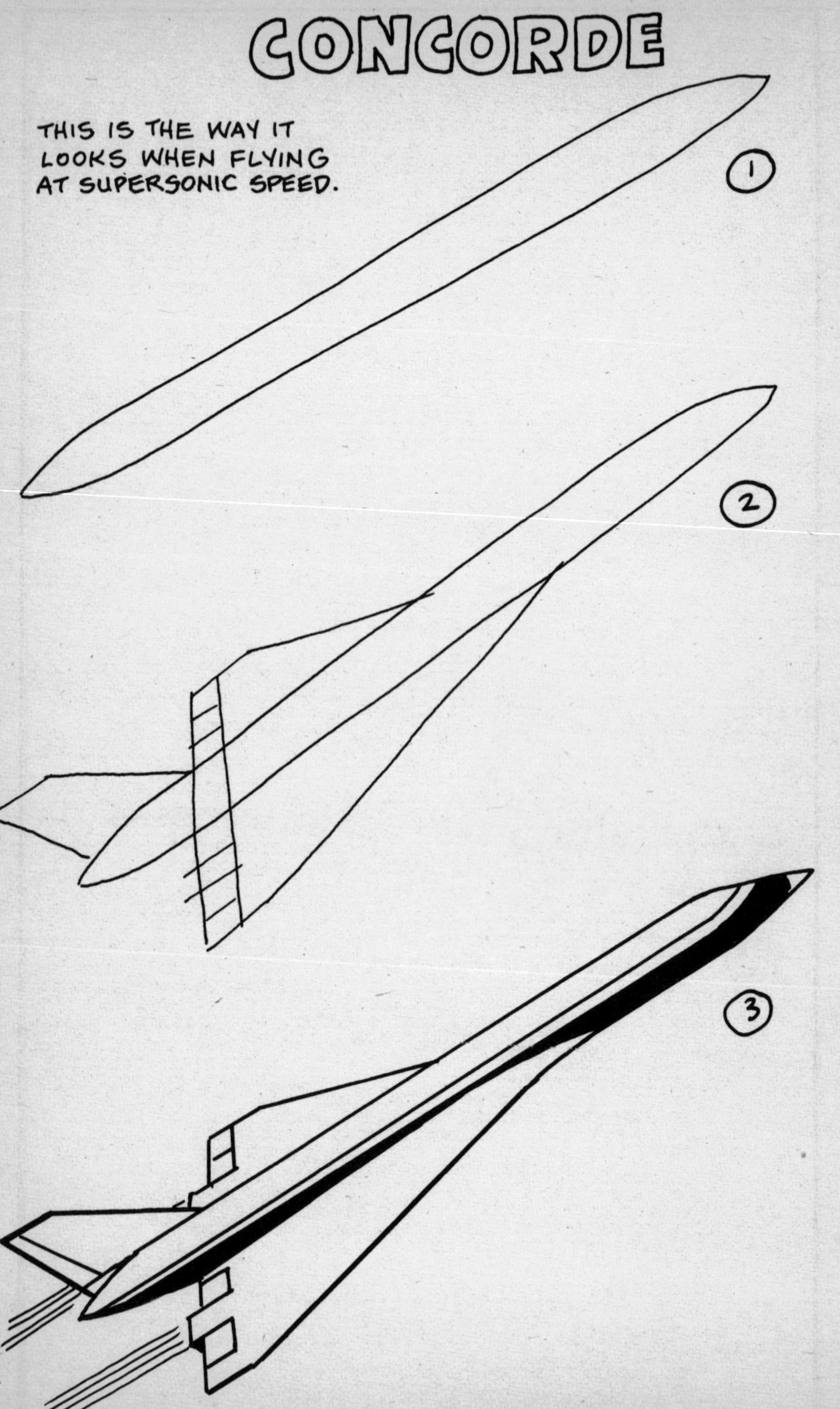
CONCORDE
THIS IS THE WAY IT
LOOKS WHEN FLYING
AT SUPERSONIC SPEED.
1
2
3

CONCORDE

THIS IS HOW IT LOOKS DURING TAKE-OFF AND LANDING.

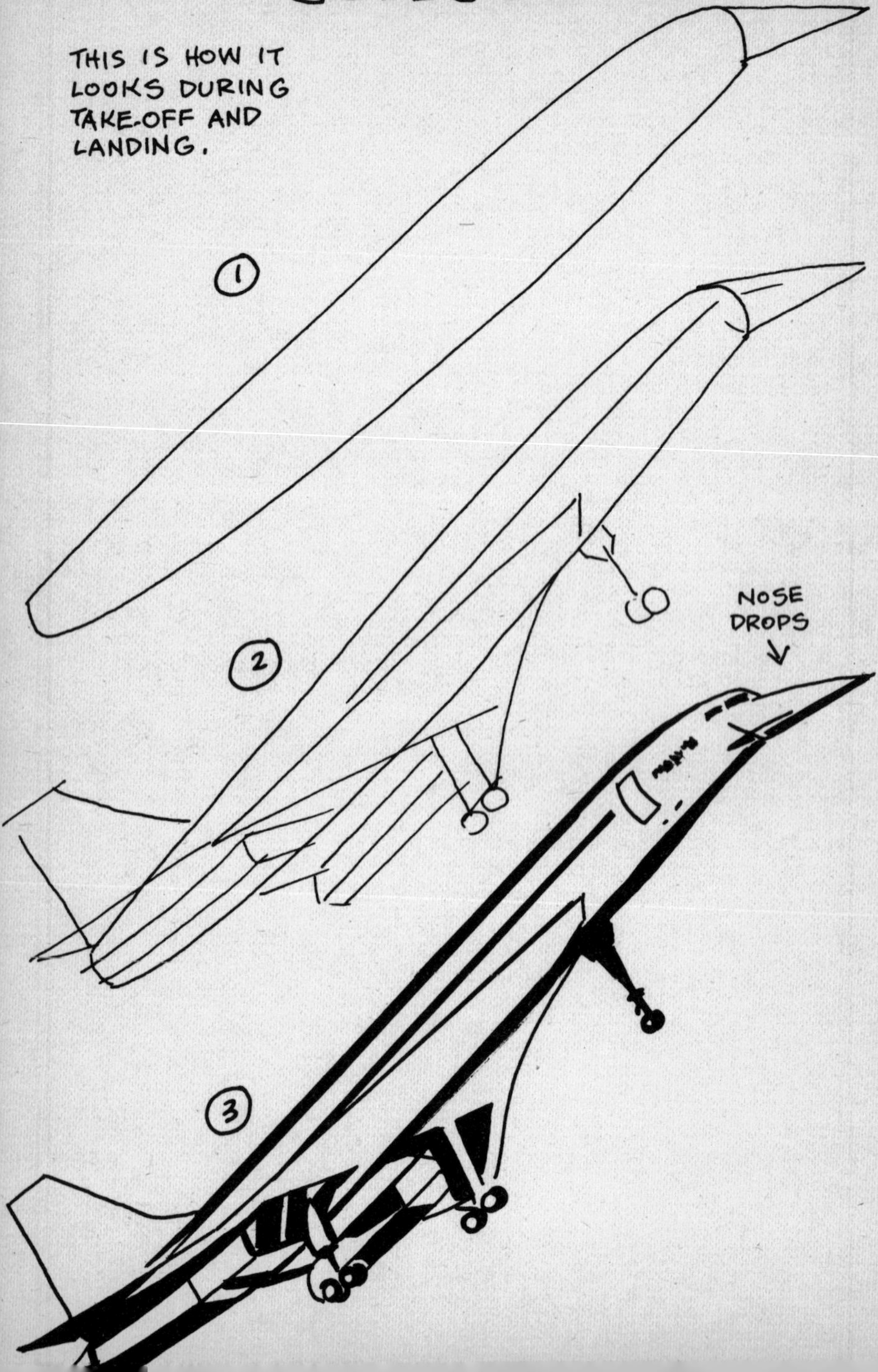

1

2

NOSE DROPS

3

LEAR JET

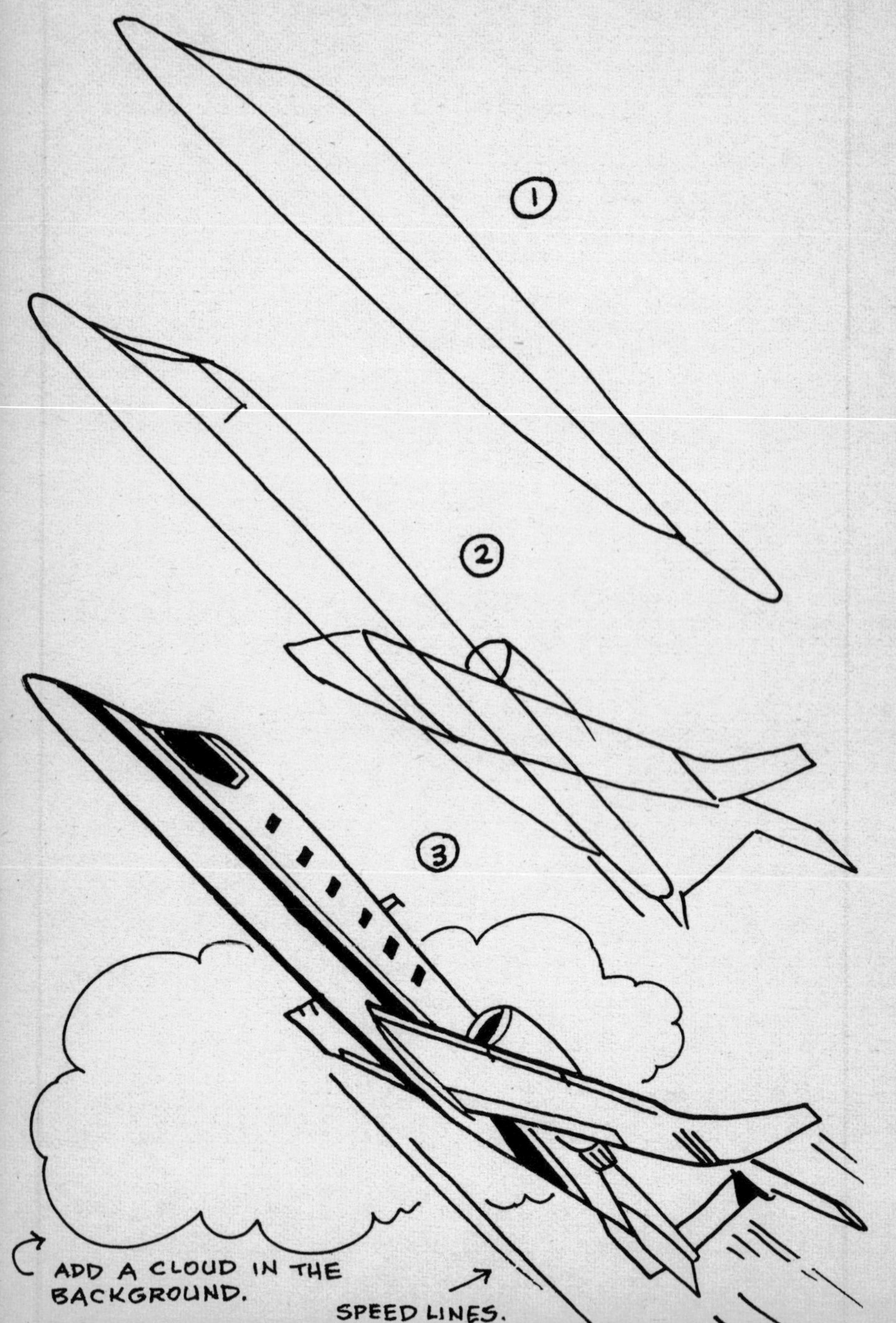

DRAW YOUR PICTURE HERE

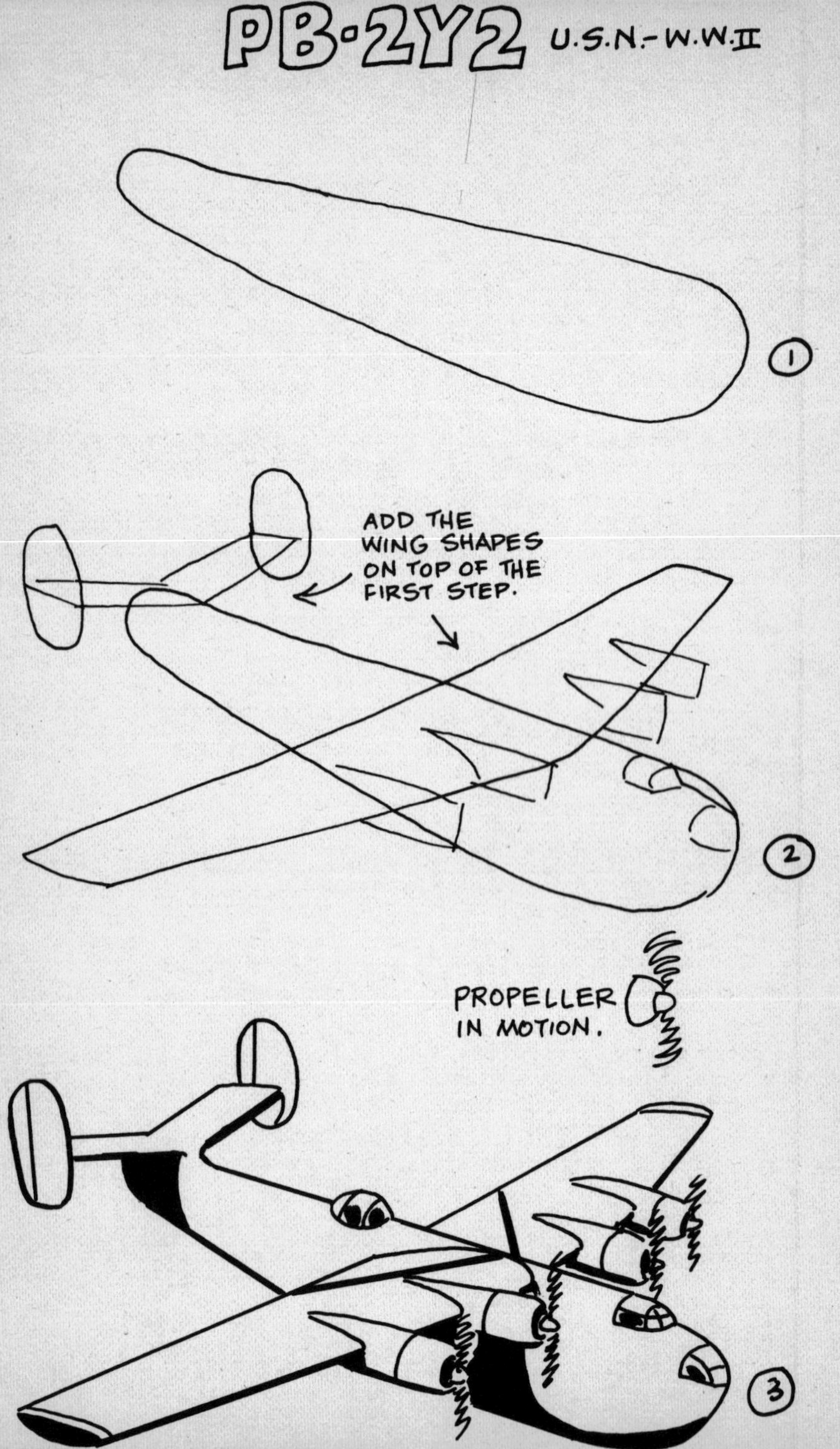
PB-2Y2 U.S.N.-W.W.II
1
ADD THE
WING SHAPES
ON TOP OF THE
FIRST STEP.
2
PROPELLER
IN MOTION.
3

DRAW YOUR PICTURE [illegible]

DH4 BRITISH-W.W.I

DRAW YOUR PICTURE HERE

FLYING BOXCAR

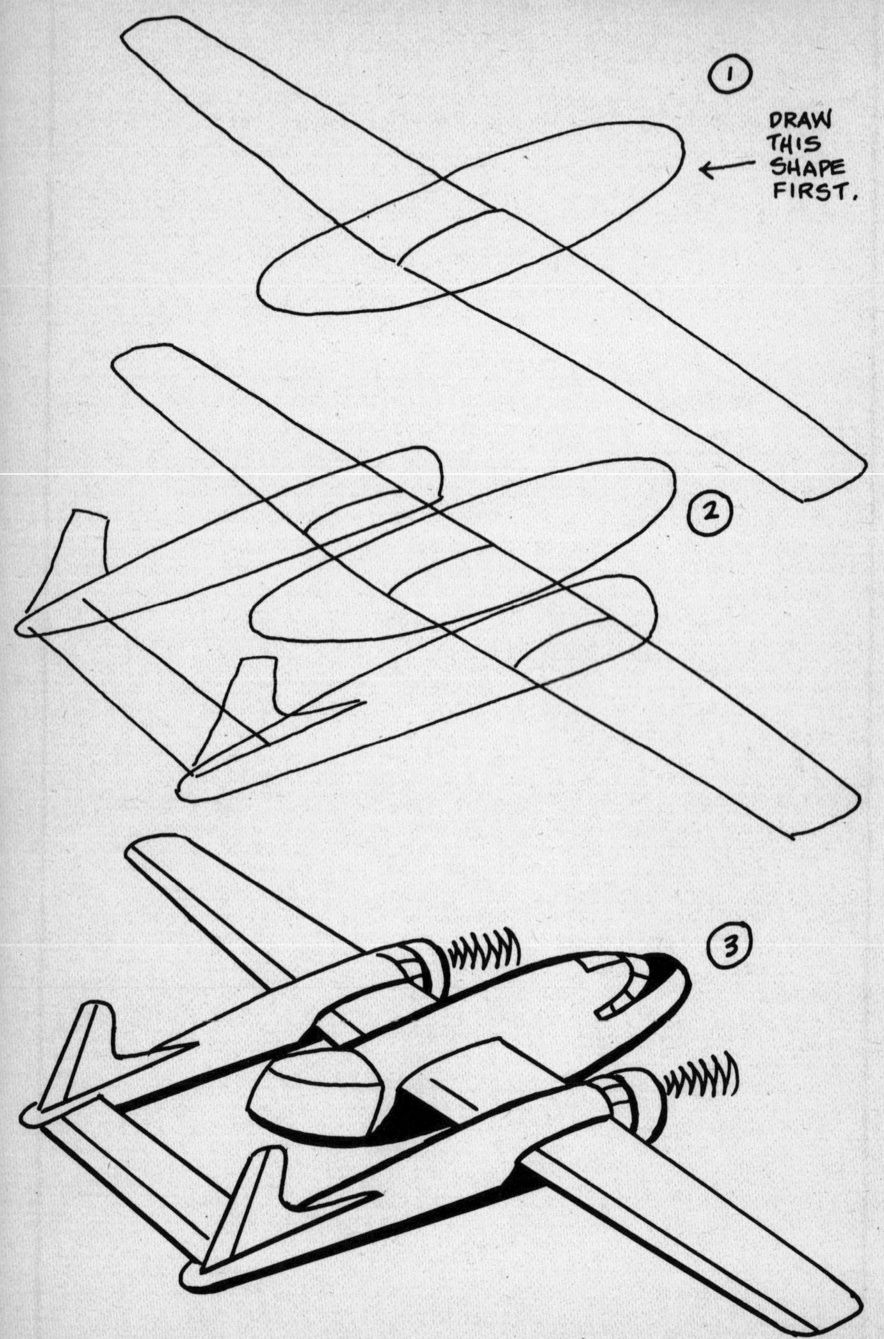

DRAW YOUR PICTURE HERE

707

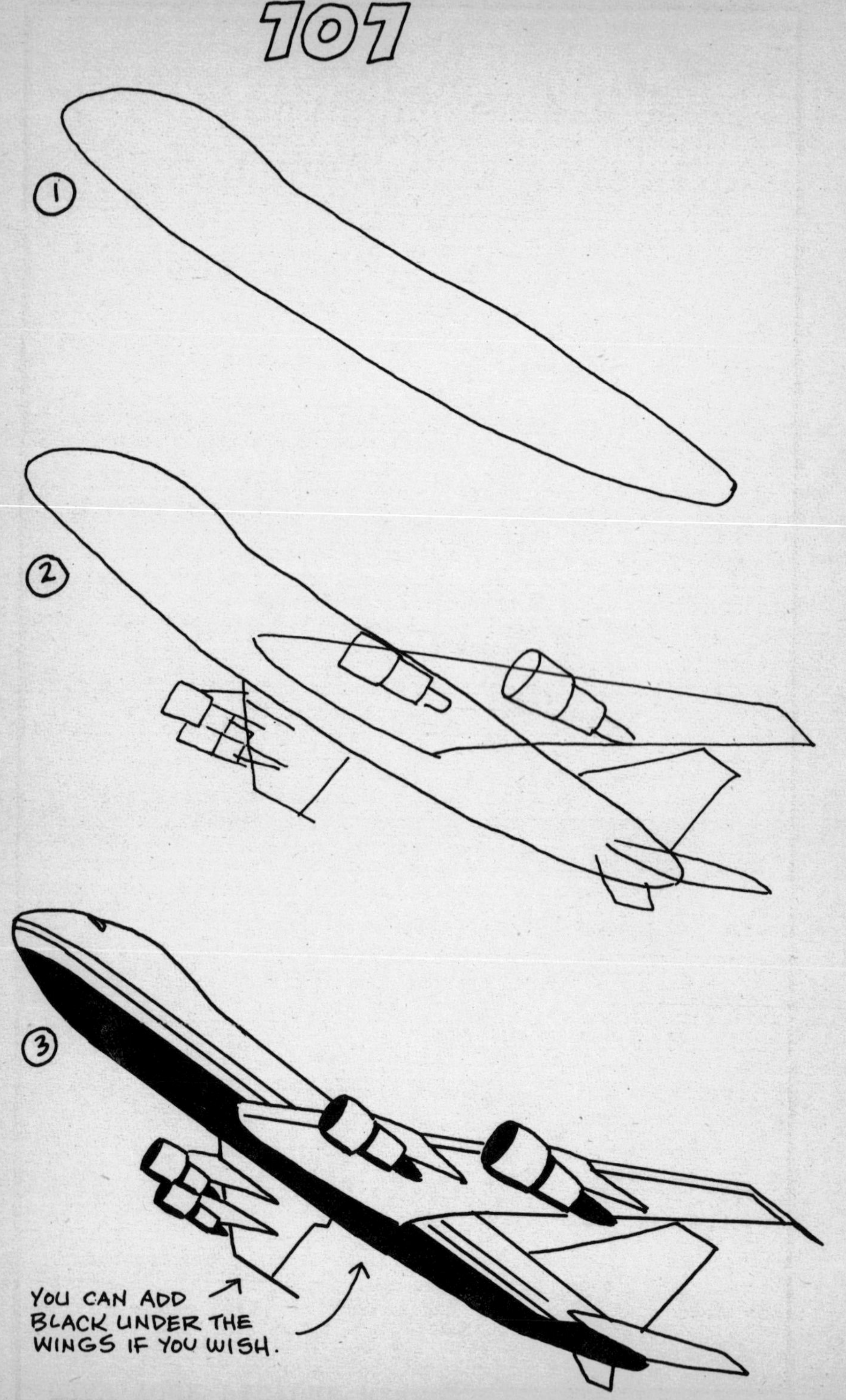

SPIRIT OF ST. LOUIS

①

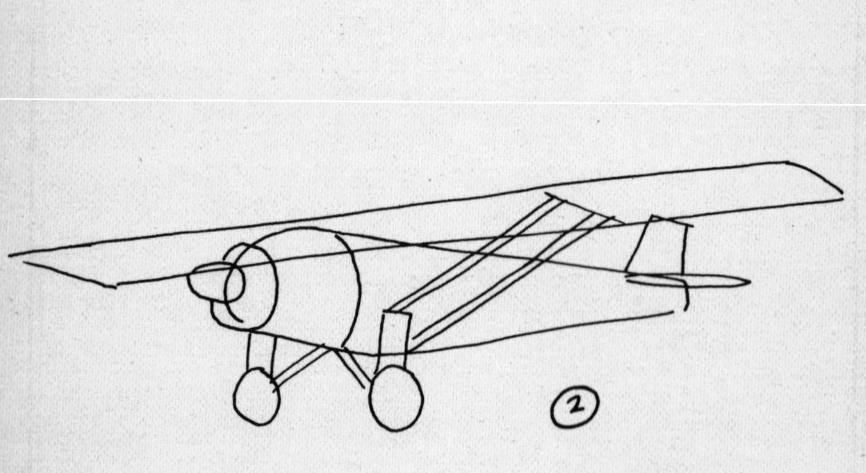

DRAW YOUR PICTURE HERE

747

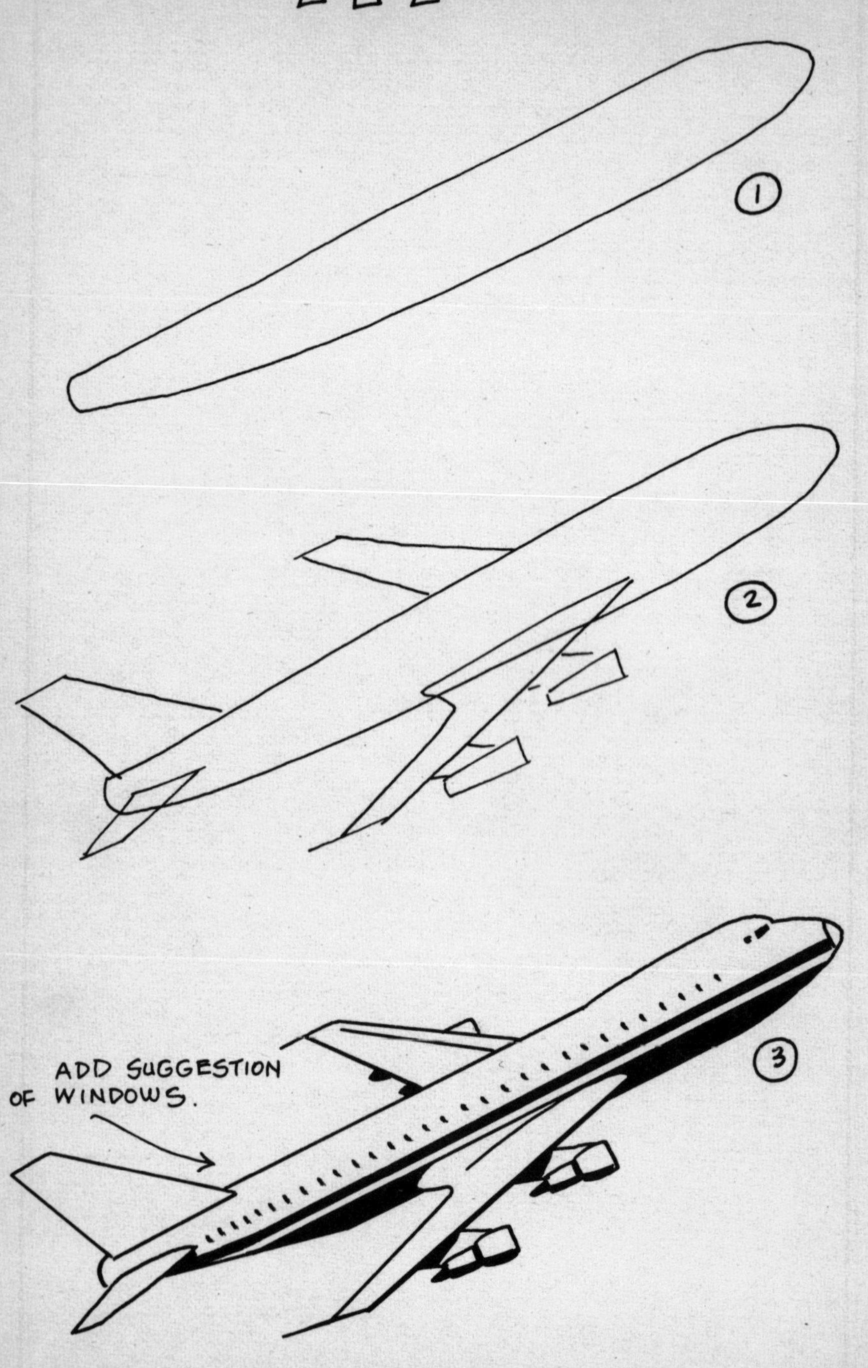

DRAW YOUR PICTURE HERE

F-14 TOMCAT

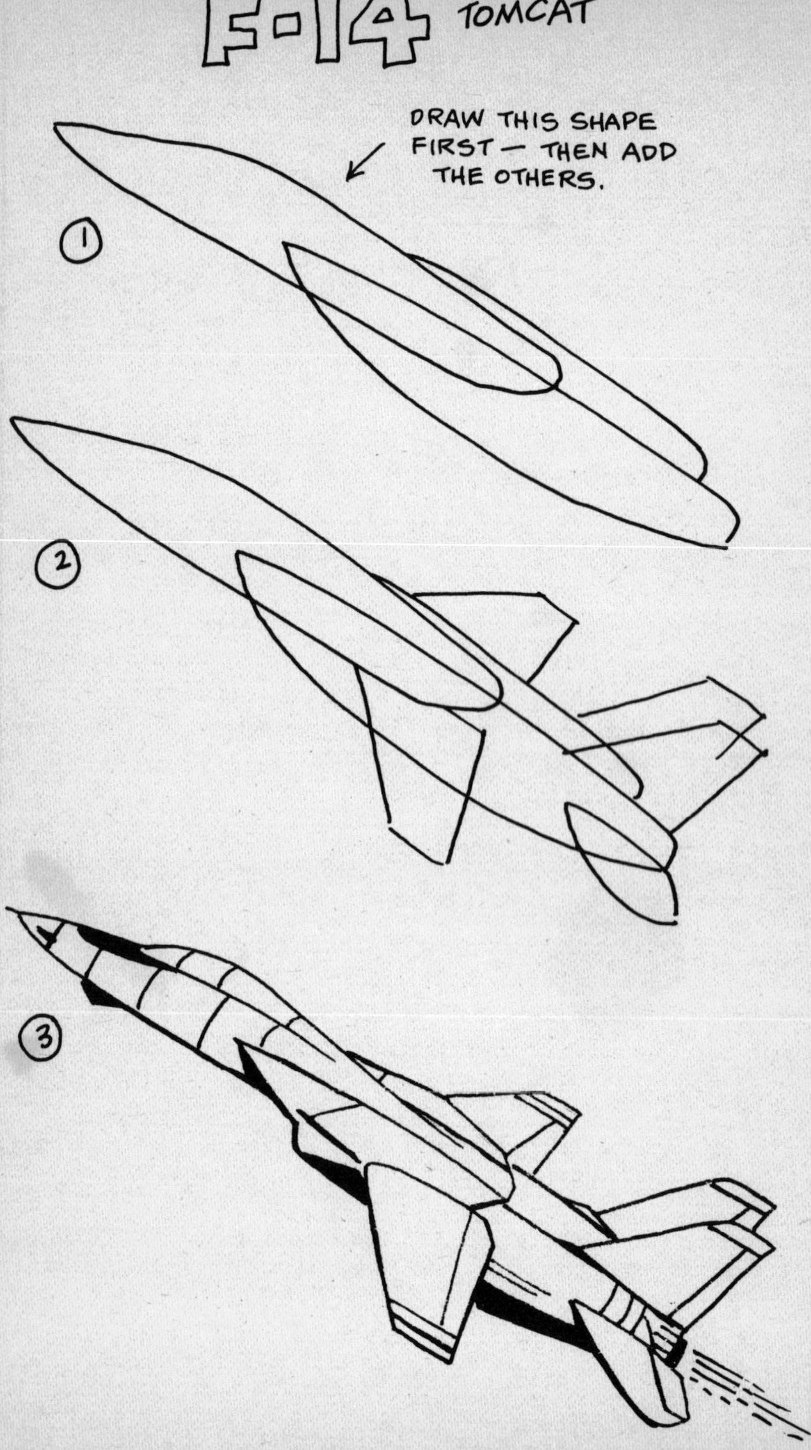

DRAW YOUR PICTURE HERE

CORSAIR U.S.-W.W.II

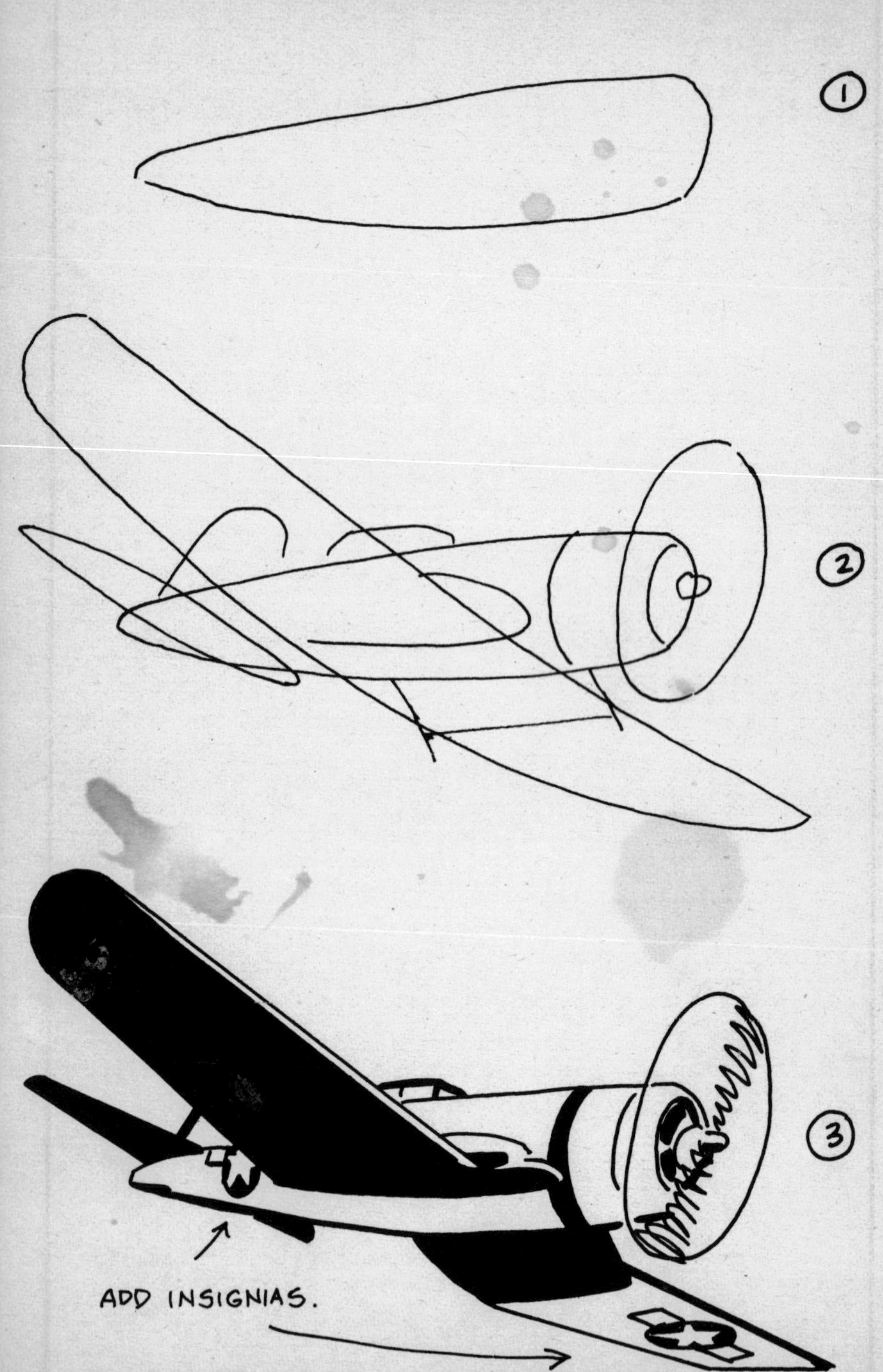

DRAW YOUR PICTURE HERE

X-1

FIRST PLANE TO FLY FASTER THAN SPEED OF SOUND.

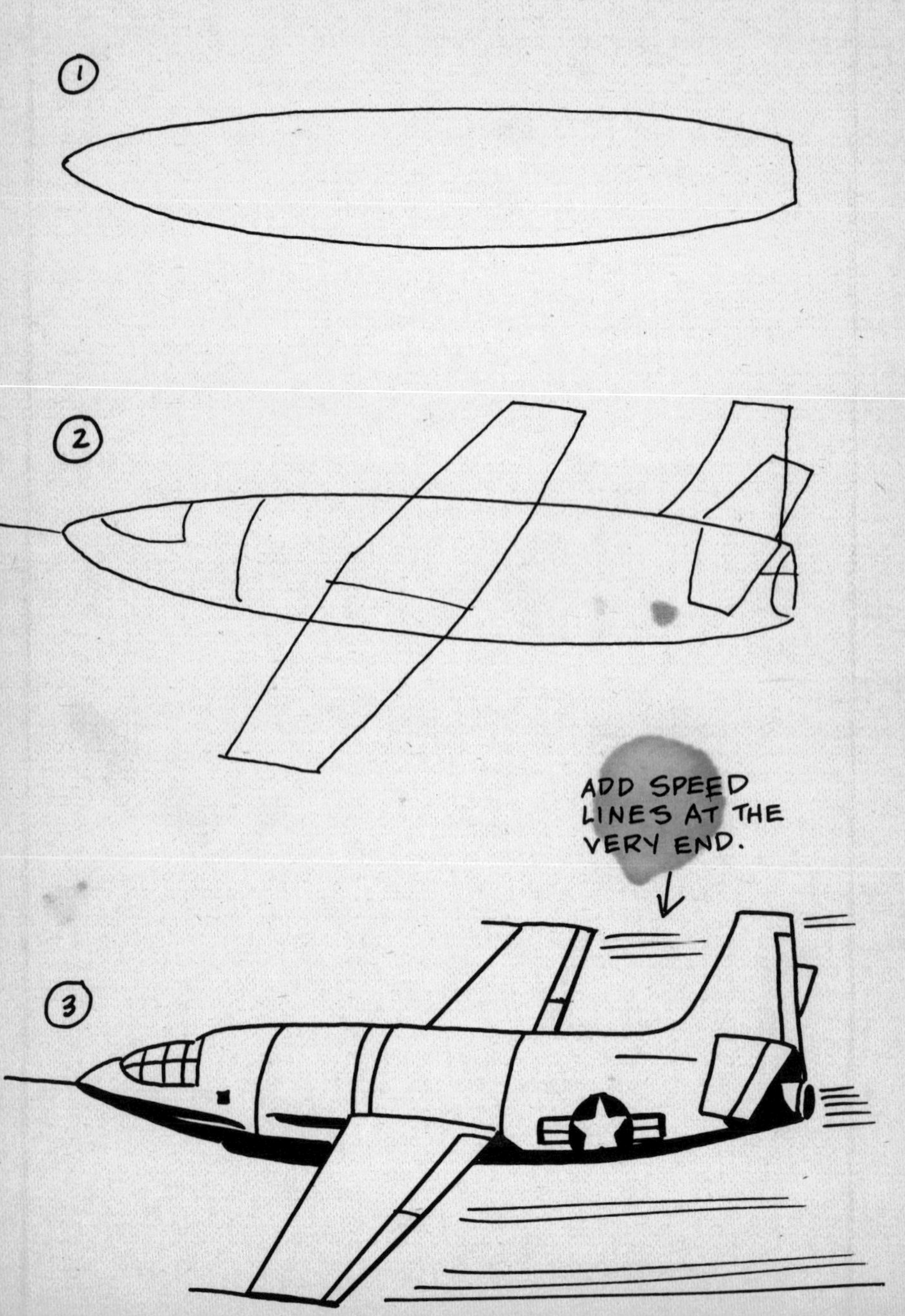

DRAW YOUR PICTURE HERE

DC-9

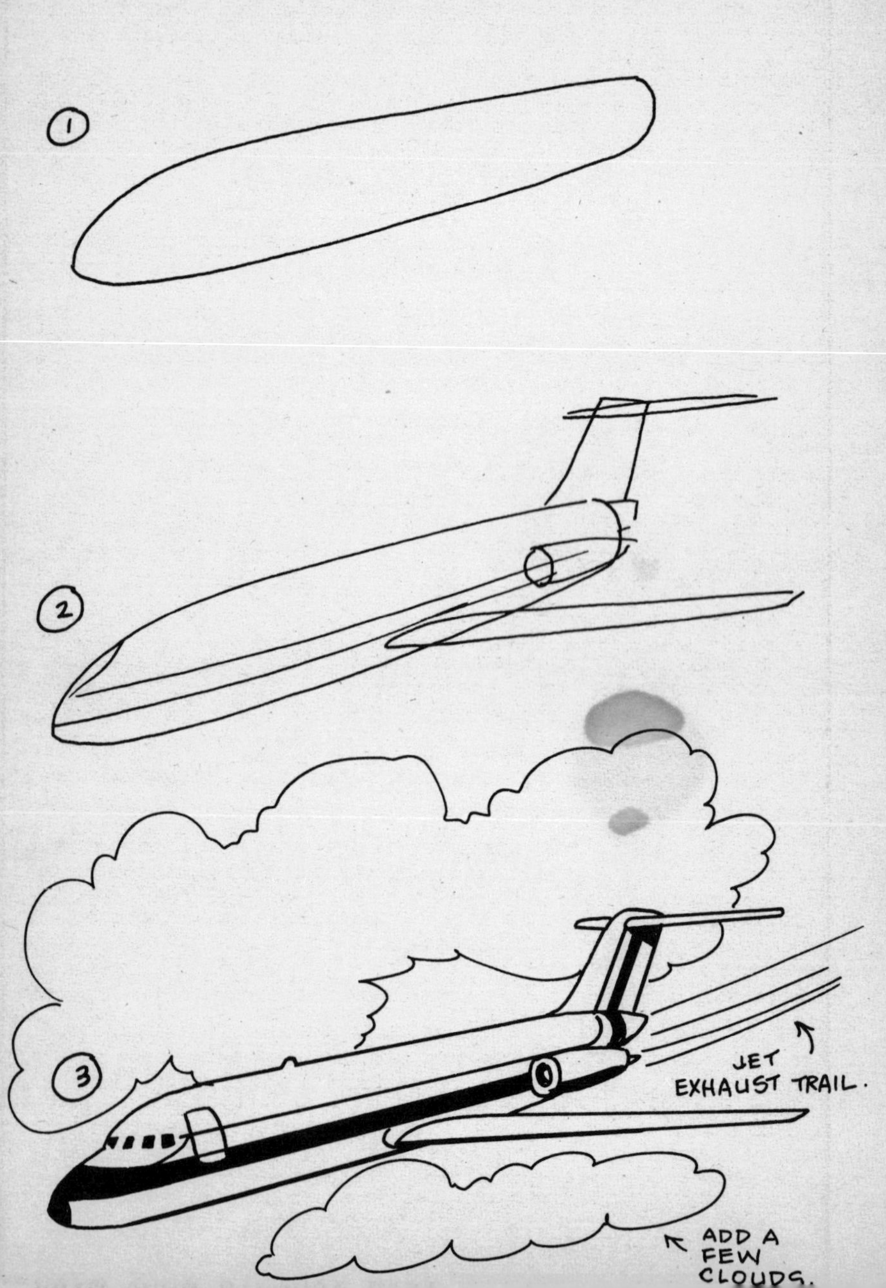

DRAW YOUR PICTURE HERE

GRUMMAN HELLCAT

U.S.-W.W.II

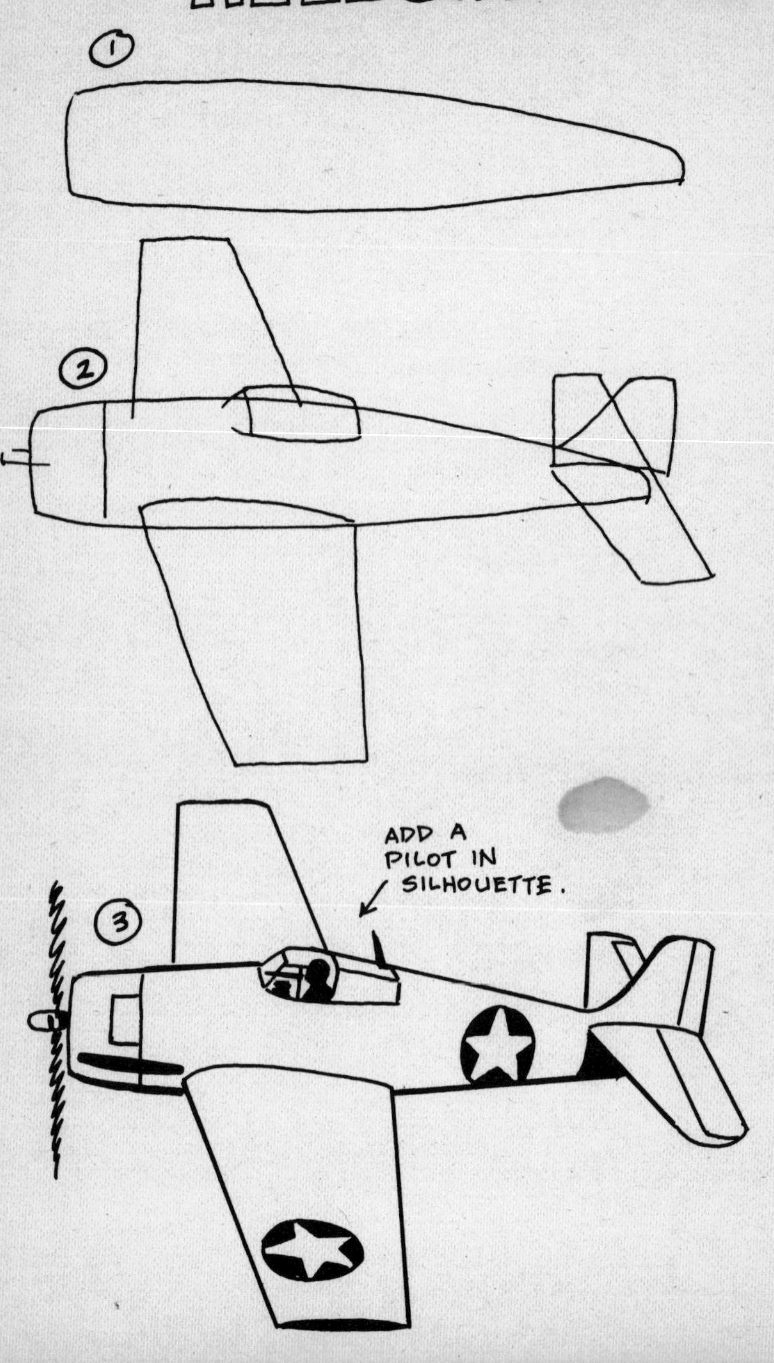

DRAW YOUR PICTURE HERE

STEALTH BOMBER

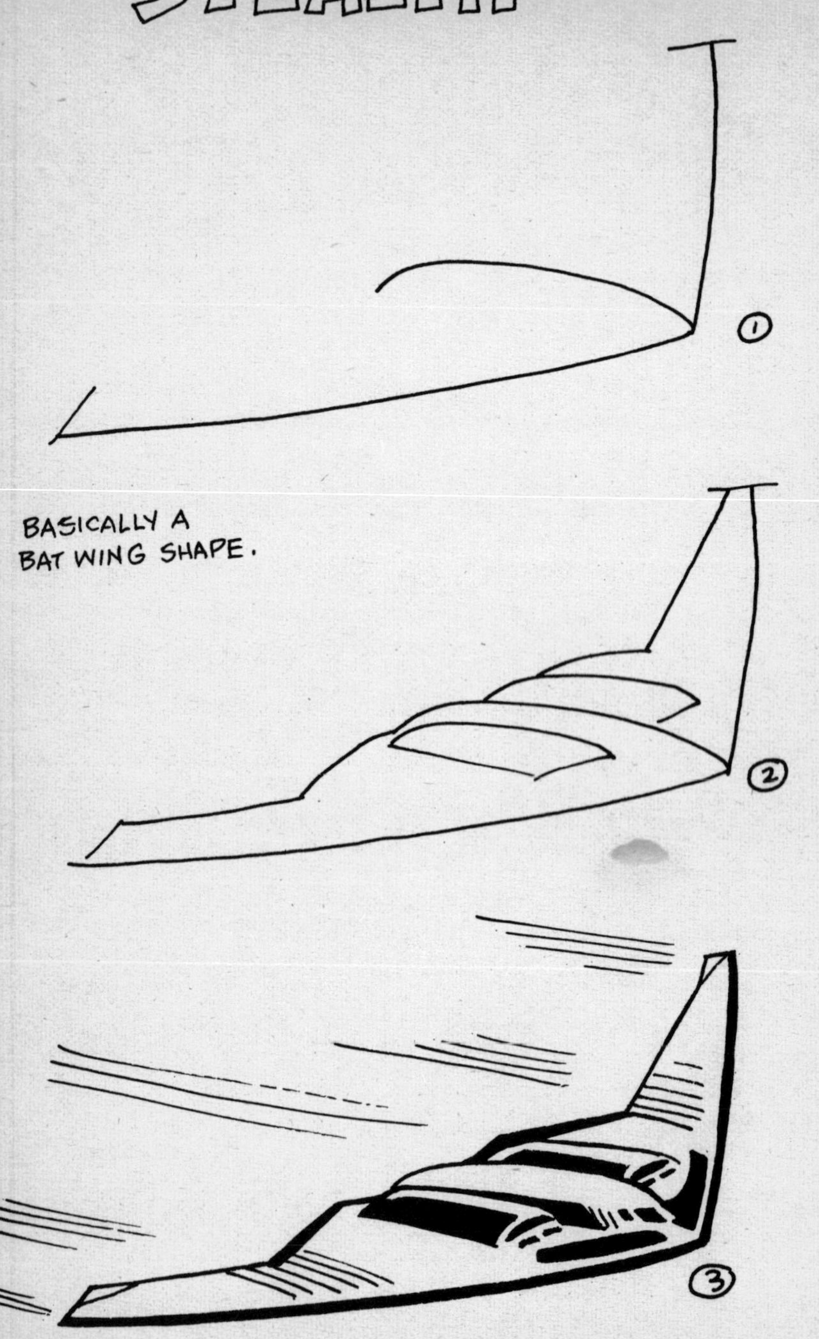

F-18 HORNET

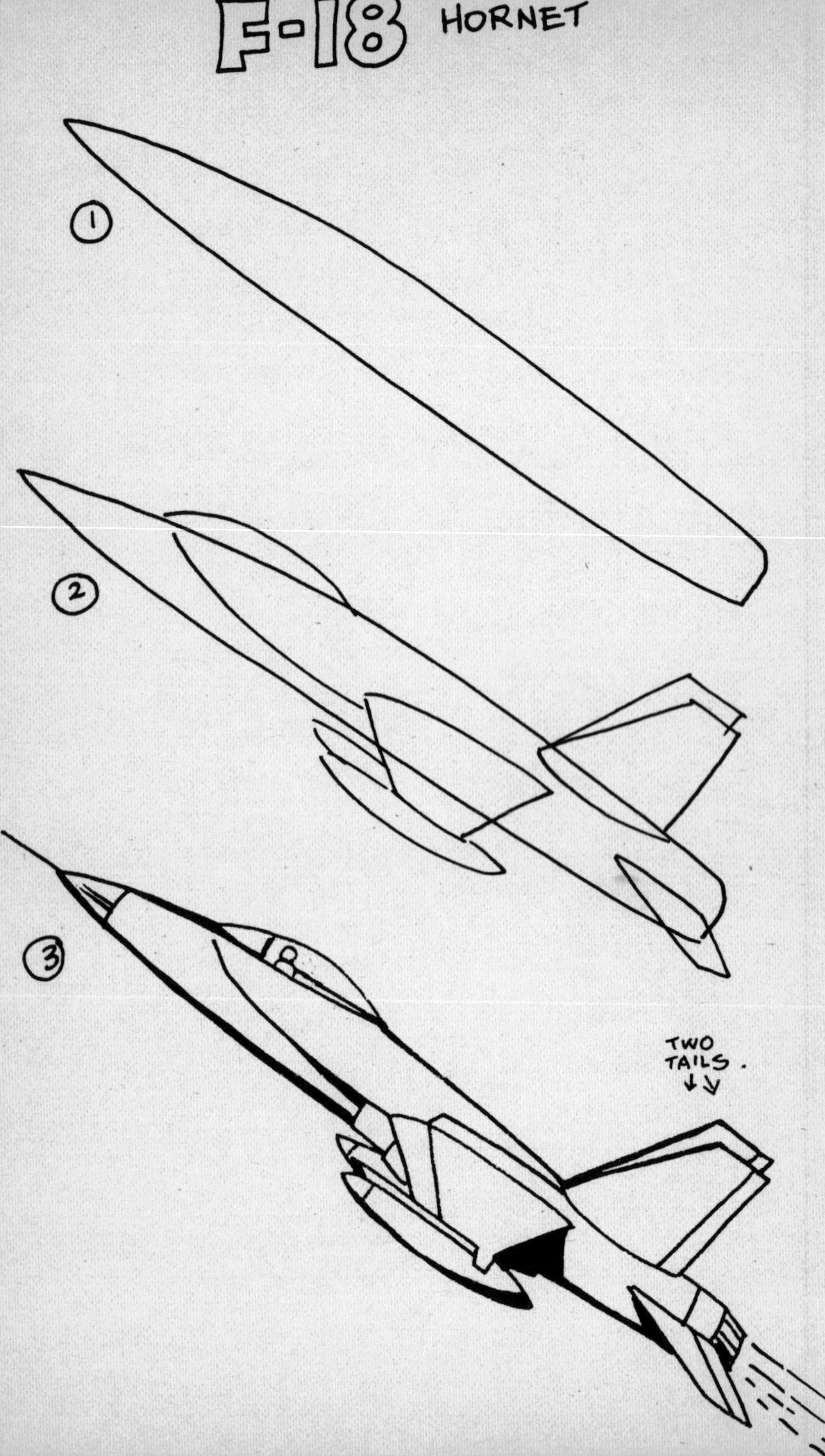

DRA YOUR PICTURE HERE

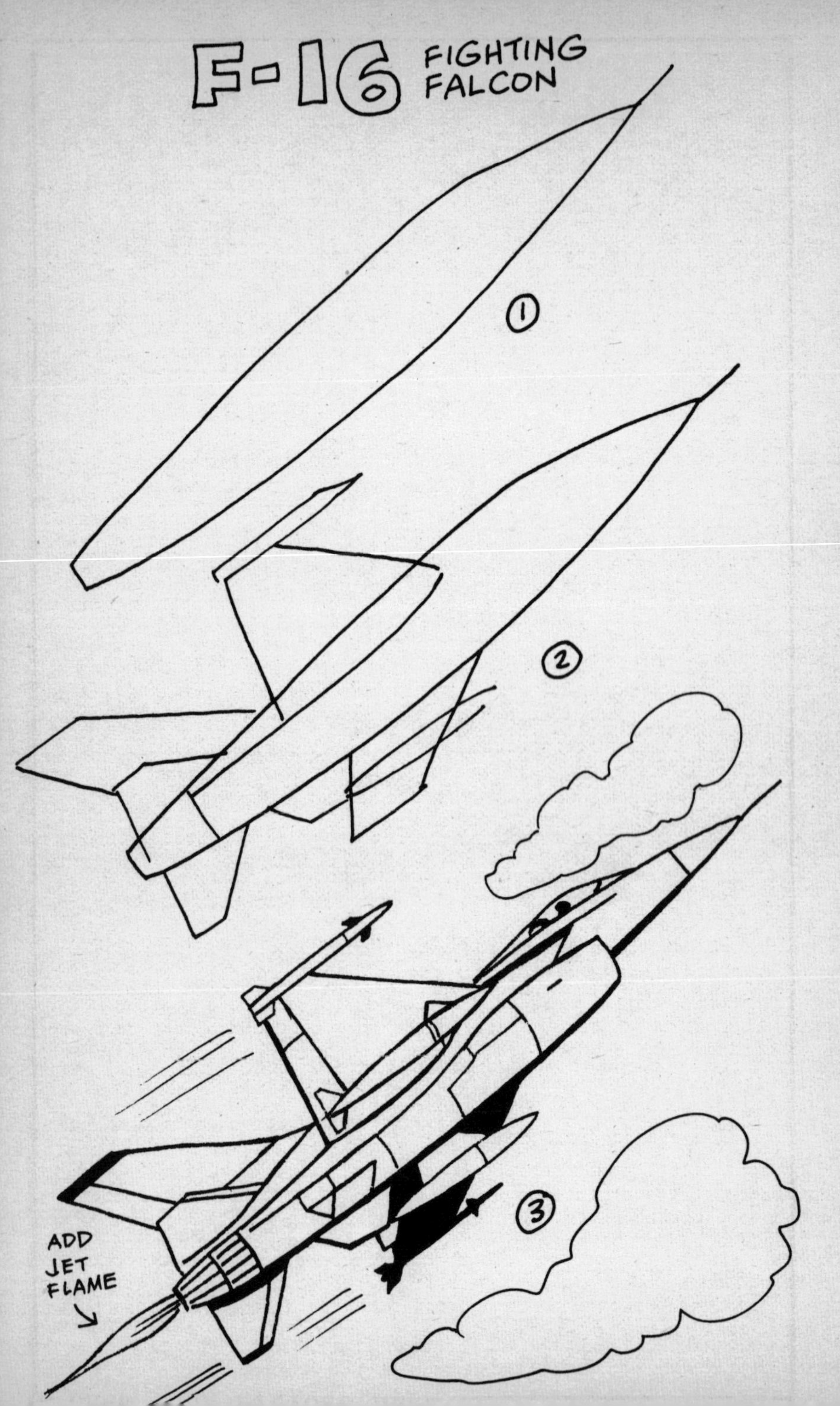
F-16
FIGHTING FALCON
1
2
3
ADD JET FLAME

B-52

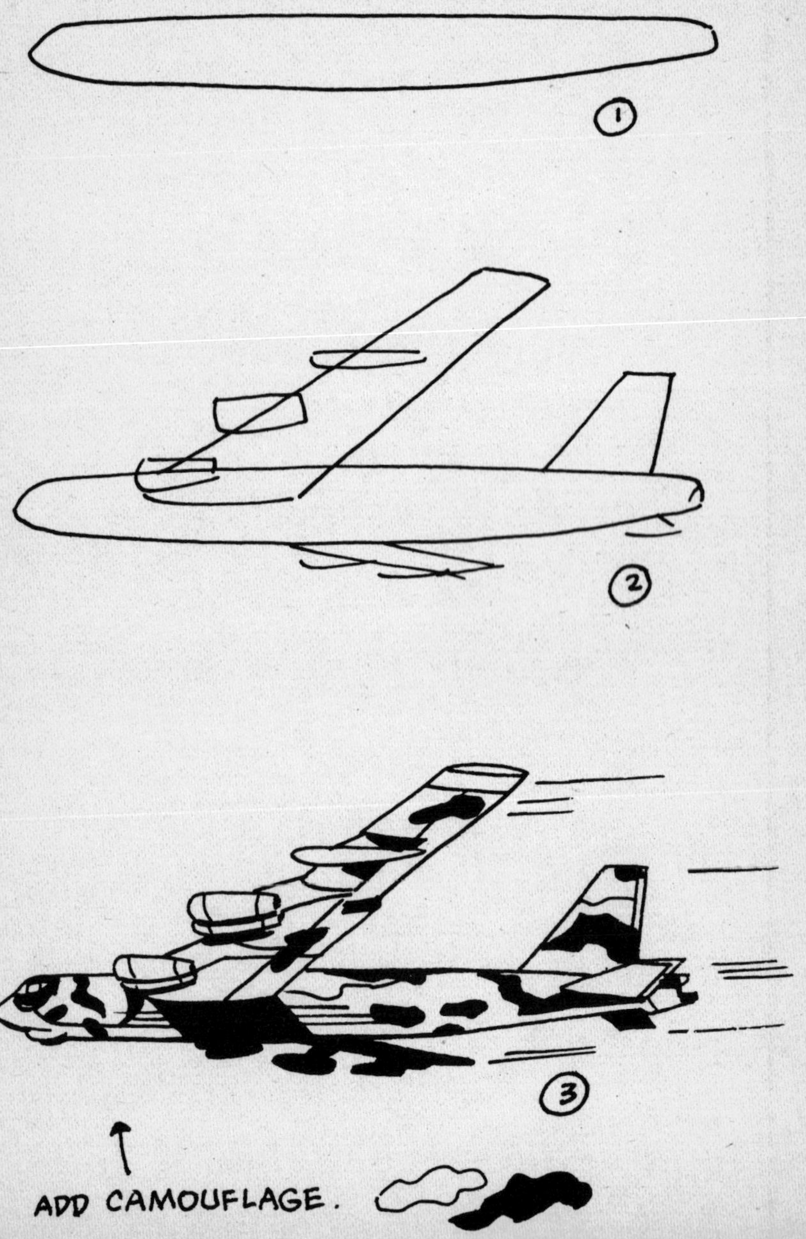

VTOL
(VERTICAL TAKE-OFF & LANDING)

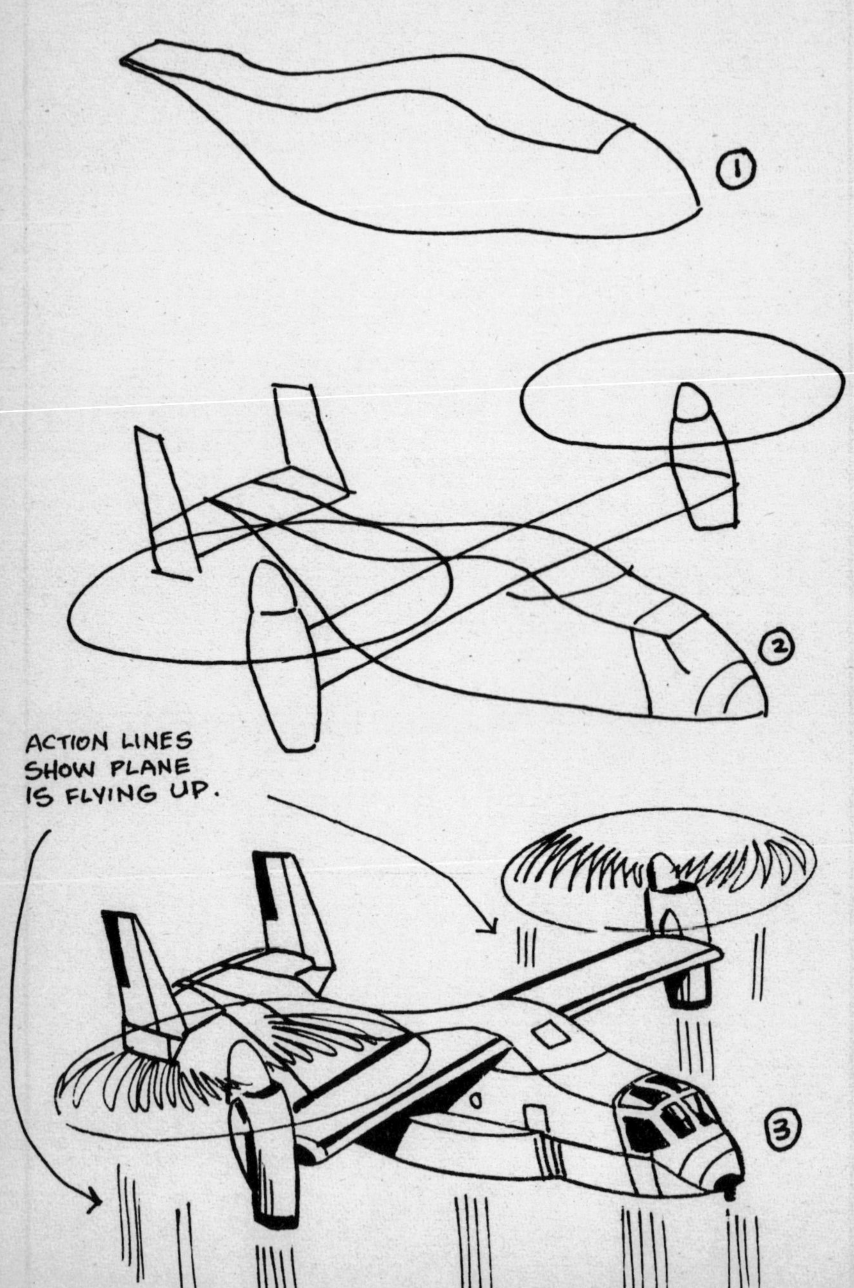

DRAW YOUR PICTURE HERE

SPACE SHUTTLE

1

2

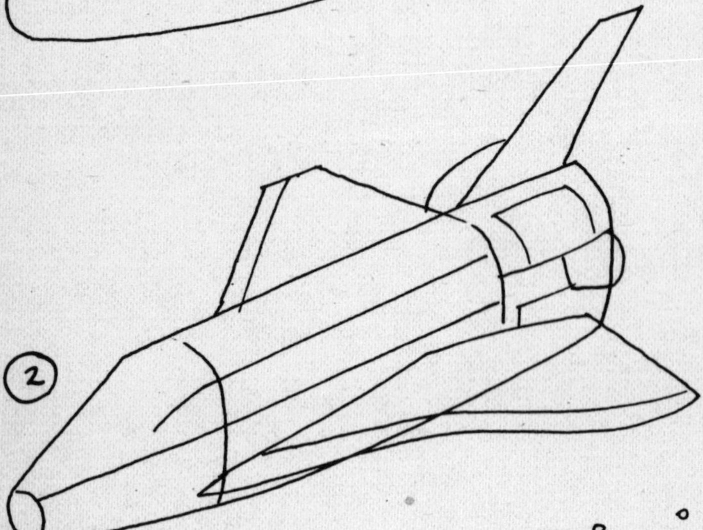

ADD STARS AND PLANETS.

3

DRAW YOUR FAVORITE AIRPLANE HERE —